Bullet Points
Volume 6

Paperback edition, first impression, July 2024
ISBN 979-8-2271737-6-8
© 2024 BULLET POINT PRESS, to the extent specified in publication agreements with authors. All rights reserved.

The Arabic block *noon* colophon is a trademark of BULLET POINT PRESS.

Cover design by Nathan W. Toronto. Cover © 2024 Nathan W. Toronto. Cover image by likozor (used under license). Interior design by Nathan W. Toronto using the Spectral LaTeX font.

Other editions: ISBN 979-8-3331415-5-2 (paperback) | ISBN 979-8-2233204-5-6 (electronic) | ASIN B0D9FYYIWJ (electronic)

BULLET POINTS VOLUME 6

Nathan W. Toronto
Editor

BULLET POINT PRESS

*For those who come back from war
and fight battles we cannot see.*

Emory Upton and Science Fiction

THE TRUISM THAT THOSE WHO FIGHT hate war the most bears repeating. It is one of the driving mantras of *Bullet Points*, giving the lie to the unfounded bias against military science fiction, that those who read and write it must somehow glorify violence or support war. *Bullet Points* aims to contribute to a world where war is less likely because all people hate it as much as those who must fight.

No one embodies this ethic more than Emory Upton, the U.S. Army officer who graduated from West Point just two months after the attack on Fort Sumter and who after the Civil War catalyzed the reforms that put the U.S. military on a footing to help win two world wars. He was promoted to the rank of brevet major general on the basis of tactical brilliance and perceptive leadership. As far as the record shows, he bore no interest in science fiction, or even in literary fiction, but he harbored an intense curiosity about changes in warfare and weaponry, and in how to make sense of the chaos and horror of war.

As warfare changes before our eyes in Ukraine, Gaza, Sudan, Myanmar, and elsewhere, writers of military science fiction must keep up. Assuming that warfare in the future will somehow look the same as that of yesteryear shows a lack of inquisitiveness about the military science fiction medium, like a sculptor thinking that clay will never change or the physicist that all we know about the universe has already been discovered.

War is terrible, it is "hell," as one of Upton's commanders famously averred. But this does not mean that speculative military fiction should shy from its horrors and tragedy. The evils of war have also produced human hope and honor that, while they certainly do not redeem war's evils, nonetheless suggest that war can also produce goodness. War is one of humanity's oldest institutions. We must understand both its evils and its goodness better if we are to make it less thinkable.

This is the point that Upton understood so tragically. Raised a strict millenarian Protestant in the aftermath of the eighteenth-century Great Awakening, Upton lost his faith after the horrors of Fredericksburg and Salem during the Civil War. He thereafter worked with assiduous fanaticism to improve tactics, education, and officership in the Army so that the future would not witness the profligate waste of good men that he witnessed in combat, in a war where over 600,000 American combatants lost their lives, to say nothing of the untold civilians who suffered and died.

The tragedy of Upton's life is that the horrors of war never truly left him. He lost the wife he dearly loved to a debilitating illness and he died, childless, from suicide in 1881, likely the victim of brain tumors. His military brilliance was unrivaled, having risen to commandant of cadets at West Point and having written the definitive analysis of military education and training around the world in the years after the formative Franco-Prussian War.

The after-battle that the Civil War left him with surely contributed to the premature end to a stellar military career and an impactful life, which is why this volume of *Bullet Points* is dedicated to those whose wars don't end after the shooting trails off in wisps of cordite and spent steel. If we in military science fiction, like Upton, can understand war and warfare even marginally better than we did yesterday, then we will have done some small service and created goodness from horror.

If we give a leg up to a few old soldiers along the way, all the better.

—Nathan W. Toronto, ed.

CONTENTS

The Owl's Last Call

K. M. RIDER

By day, K. M. Rider writes marketing communications and website content for nonprofit and health/medical organizations. After dark, she crafts stories that reveal the extraordinary and mystical that lie within mundane moments and ordinary lives. Her short fiction has been published in *Strange: An Anthology of Speculative Fiction* and her freelance work has appeared in an assortment of digital and print publications. She has no military experience, except that of Major Mom. "The Owl's Last Call" is original to *Bullet Points*.

WHISKEY AND BEER BOTTLES CLINK as they spin across the cedar deck. A chill breeze rouses Angello. He turns over on the rickety hammock where he crashed the night before, and has wasted away most of another day.

"Wooh-hu, wooh-hu. Wooh-hu, wooh-hu."

"That damn owl!"

Angello jolts to his feet. Muscles in his back spasm around the shrapnel—pieces of war—embedded inside him, forever. Leaning against the porch frame, his eyes search for the owl in the trees behind his cabin.

Dawn and dusk, even in his dreams, the owl's deep, resonant call haunts him.

Suddenly, with the stealth of a silent assassin, the owl swoops past the screened porch. Angello watches it dive into tall grasses at the edge of the woods. Its talons swing forward, opening into two razor sharp, four-pronged claws. Moments later, the owl emerges with a young fox caught in its talons and brings it into the clearing behind the cabin. Mantling its prey with an erect stance and wings spread wide, the owl resembles a shaman wearing a flowing tawny brown and black cloak. The fox writhes in the owl's grip. Without hesitation the owl jabs its black beak into the fox's head. The kill is precise, quick and, unlike the killing Angello has witnessed, done with mercy.

Angello rubs his bald head. A freight train of a headache is tunneling between his temples. He gulps down a can of flat Coke. The last time he was on a drinking binge this bad was during those first weeks back from the Second Afghanistan War. If it wasn't for the IED that took his lower right leg and seared his body with enough shrapnel to sound a metal detector, he might still be with his Marine brothers. Instead, his life had slipped into a civilian shithole.

IN THE SIXTEEN MONTHS since he had returned home from his fifth and final active duty tour, Angello just couldn't deal with people . . . at least not regular people who knew nothing about making life-and-death decisions. All around him were people—people who loved him, people who knew him from his life before the wars, and complete strangers—who wanted to do for him, give to him, help him deal with what happened "over there." They wanted to know everything Angello wanted to forget.

It was easier for him to lock it all down inside. But memories like his were a slow-killing poison . . . no one is aware of the damage being done until it's too late. Jobless, nearly broke, and emotionally broken, Angello now faced losing the one person he thought he'd never let slip away from him—the woman he's loved since high school—Shaila.

"Wooh-hu. wooh-hu."

Perched atop Angello's motorcycle, the owl turns its head until its fiery amber eyes lock on Angello.

"Son of a bitch! If I get my hands on you, I'll make your head really spin."

The screen door snaps from the hinge and hangs lopsided in the rusted frame as Angello hurriedly limps to his bike. The owl is already in the trees, watching. Thin streaks of blood from the recent kill remain where the owl had wrapped its talons around the handlebars. Angello notices the time on the mounted clock: 3:26 p.m.

Damn. Shaila's flight to London is tonight. I still can't believe she's going. She'll be leaving for the airport by 4:30 p.m.

SHAILA. Being with her should have been easy. But it wasn't. Even so, from that first kiss in high school and all the years that intervened, no matter whom they had taken to bed or how much distance came between them, they couldn't untangle themselves from each other. But the sands of Afghanistan had scarred him, repeatedly. Bad timing and lousy choices kept the aura of possibility between them from becoming something more.

No—that's bullshit. It wasn't any of that. It was him.

"Wooh-hu, wooh-hu." The owl passes low over Angello. The tip of its wing brushes the top of his head.

It's now or never.

He swings his leg over the saddle, loses balance and the bike nearly takes him down. He recovers quickly and steadies the heavy bike, only because he had the dumb luck of qualifying for the Stark Edition Neuroprosthetic that replaced his lower leg.

He pulls the helmet over his head and slides the visor down. The gruff engine fires up with raw authority. Dust kicks up into a funnel behind him as he pulls the bike onto Route 44 east toward Avian Mountain.

The late-afternoon autumn sun beats through Angello's bomber jacket. Accelerating up the incline in the shadow of Avian's tiered, western-facing cliffs, knobs and peaks loom like sentries guarding the river valley. He takes no notice of the cliff-side panorama that had once made him feel as if he could ride off the edge and soar into the hands of God. Angello stopped believing in God that day in what was left of Helmand Province, Afghanistan. He wrestles back the memory, focusing instead on the steep climb, and anticipating the switchbacks on the other side of the mountain.

Coming around the first turn at the peak, dark clouds roll across the sky. Icy, bluish mist descends upon the road. Raindrops pelt Angello's helmet and the demon-memory breaks through. His mind flashes to the sandpit, to the explosion that took the lives of four SpecOps Marines, including his best friend Mike.

THAT DAY HAD STARTED just the same as any other in the scorching heat of the dawning summer in the Province. They were on patrol all night, crammed into a JLTV, each man wearing one hundred pounds of gear and ammo and overcome by a hot, hazy fugue that could be sparked to clarity in the blink of an eye.

At daybreak, they deployed the vehicle to secure a small brick building in an abandoned village. Angello hung back to call in coordinates as the other guys proceeded toward the objective. Not that much about these security checks had changed from the First Afghanistan War.

The call-in takes only a minute. The guys are ahead, maybe by ten yards, approaching the entrance. Suddenly, the sand vibrates beneath Angello's boots. *Boom!* Blinding flashes of orange light. Angello's legs buckle beneath him. Heat, sand, and debris from the blast burst into the air and smother him in thick, gray smoke. Bodies, hurled from the earth, drop from the sky like ragdolls. Broken and torn, there's no telling which limbs belong to which Marine.

Angello tries to scramble to his feet. He falls chest first into the solid, packed sand. His leg is charred and bloody, but there's no time to tend to his own injury. He's got to get to the other men. A quick scan and he pinpoints some of the men—but not Mike. Where the fuck is Mike?

Crawling fast and low on his belly, choking on the gritty, tinny taste of sand and blood, he reaches the Captain and Gunnery Sergeant. Their bodies lay mangled in a crater the size of a mini-Cooper. Another body is sprawled across the entryway. Angello checks the tags. It's the explosives disposal tech. The flesh of his face appears raked away as if by the hands of an unskilled butcher. Angello pulls himself up inside the doorway, readies his rifle, and checks the interior. Small bodies, women and children, are heaped in a pile in the corner of the room. A macabre tapestry of flesh and blood and bone splattered on the walls and windows.

Groans rise from the wall opposite the doorway. "Angello, that you, buddy?"

It's Mike's voice. Dragging his left leg behind him, Angello makes his way to his best friend. Mike's left arm is nothing more than bloody strips of flesh and his right leg is gone. Sunlight glints off a metal triangle projecting from his chest like the tip of an iceberg. He knows it's a lie, but Angello promises to get him out, home to his wife and newborn daughter. But you could never bullshit Magic Mike, the nickname he earned not just for his bar-top dance moves but for his uncanny ability to sense trouble before it happened. Just not this time.

"You gotta get home. Give tags . . . wife . . . my baby girl." Angello wipes blood from Mike's mouth. Tells him to save his breath. But Mike is stubborn even to his last incoherent breath. "Ang, when you . . . want . . . quit . . . hope and desire."

Angello doesn't remember calling in the casualty evacuation. He doesn't remember the steady thunder of the chopper as it descended to retrieve the dead. What he does remember is staring into Mike's eyes before reaching his hand to close the lids. He remembers that he had never noticed how his best friend's eyes weren't just brown: a halo of deep gold shimmered around the pupils and filled Mike's eyes with flecks of light. All Angello remembers is wondering, in fact he hasn't stopped wondering, why he hadn't been dealt the same fate as these men—at the least, why not him, instead of Mike.

THE MOTORCYCLE SLIPS beneath him. His thighs grip the saddle as he cuts hard into the first switchback.

Focus!

Snow mixes with the rain, reflecting in the bike's headlight like crystalline shards on the blacktop. Fog builds on his visor. He flips it up. Sleet stings his face. He turns on the radio. Static. Checks the clock. 4:07 p.m. He should've arrived at her house by now.

The wind bites at him as he takes the next turn. The back wheel fishtails. Angello leans his weight into the saddle, manipulates the brake and recovers control in time to complete the turn. Ahead, the westbound lane twists around a wall of jagged rock. Alongside the eastbound lane—the lane Angello is riding in—wooded embankments camouflage sheer cliffs that drop off to the valley below. The only thing between staying on the road and going over the edge is a steel guardrail.

Every friggin' time I try to do the right thing . . . I should've come home in a box. Maybe I should just let her go.

A shadow flashes in the headlights. The road seems to disappear in the storm. The bike hits a pothole. The front fork torques and the back of the bike kicks-up. Angello is flung into the fog blanketing the mountain. The bike flips end-over-end. The front tire breaks loose from the fender and spins into the middle of the road. The steel frame screeches across the blacktop, then crashes into the guardrail. Angello's body slams down in the icy brush of a shallow embankment below the rail.

A thin blanket of snow quickly covers Angello from head to toe like white linen over a dead body. The bike's brake light casts a red glow over his face. The neuroprosthetic leg jerks about before going limp, like the rest of his body.

Frozen in the dark undergrowth, there is perfect stillness until . . . something rustles in the leaves of the giant sycamore that looms over him.

Angello's eyelids fly open. His eyes dart around in the darkness. His hands press into the wet earth but he can't push himself up. Each shallow breath of cold air burns in his lungs. His legs refuse to bend and he wonders if the prosthetic sensors have failed or, maybe, he has broken his back.

He senses an unseen presence in the darkness. Something tickles his face. He lifts his head, heavy with the weight of the helmet. Despite the pain, he forces himself to keep looking.

"Who . . . who's there?"

Brilliant amber eyes flash in the darkness.

A spectral silhouette moves through a cluster of young evergreens as if taking shape out of the darkness itself.

"Who's out there?" he yells again into the cold.

"Help," a voice replies from the dark.

"Who said that?"

A hooded figure comes into sight in the crimson glow of the brake light. Amber eyes shine in a featureless face. Angello's body starts to ache and tense and convulse. Then, nothing. He cannot feel even the cold.

SUDDENLY HE IS FLYING away from his body. He sees it lying below like a corpse on an ancient, snowy funeral pyre.

I'm dead?

"I don't know. Are you? Maybe you were dead before the ride." The voice, resonant and penetrating, feels familiar. But there is no time for Angello to process the voice; the specter has pulled him into the vortex of memory. Blue-white light swirls around him.

Angello moves with the light at random speeds through every detail of his life, speeding up or slowing down with the intensity of his connection to any given memory. He relives conversations and feels the joy and desolation of every relationship—even those he didn't think mattered at all. He sees moments wasted in drunken nights, pointless fighting, missed connections. Doors he refused to open and help he refused to accept. In the tempest of space and time, he senses that every second of life, every action and every failure to act—is known and recorded.

Angello looks around the illuminated space that surrounds them. "This is some kind of freakin' bad dream or something."

"There is no insignificance." The specter shifts around Angello, its cloak billowing in the strange ether that holds them suspended in time. "Everything is a source of creative or destructive power for which each soul, including yours, is accountable."

Angello looks down at his body, still lying in the snow.

"And why should I give a shit? No one's ever answered this dumb grunt's prayers."

The specter lets out a haunting laugh. "You've never even believed prayers were heard, let alone answered."

Angello looks up at the thing with the glowing eyes, tries to see beneath the hooded cloak.

"How do you know what I believe? Just 'cause you flash my life before my eyes makes you an expert? Who the hell do you think you are?"

"You already know who I was." The voice becomes even more familiar to Angello.

"What did you say?"

"Ang, open your eyes. See what's right in front of you. There's hope and desire left in you, man. That's where you draw strength from when you want to quit."

With surprise in his eyes, Angello sees the specter for what—who—it really is.

His best friend appears to him like a holographic image, at once human, then ethereal, and with the bend of the light, one in the same.

"Mike. Oh shit, Mike. I am so sorry . . ." And for only the second time in his life, Angello's body trembles in the same way it did the day he saw the light leave Mike's eyes, with fear and awe. "If there was anything I could've done, any way for it to have been me, not you . . ."

"Give it a rest. That's not why I've been sent. Much as it sucked for me then, what happened in the Province can't be changed. This is about you . . . and Shaila. You've got a choice . . . and a chance. And somewhere inside you, you know that, otherwise why bother rushing to Shaila at the last minute?"

"That's why you're here? Mike, it's obvious she's better off without me. Isn't that why I crashed? Aren't you my escort to, um, wherever the hell the dead go?"

"Escort, I wish. They've got it easy. You're not going anywhere with me.

"Now, listen up. You can't quit. Not on yourself and not on Shaila. She gets you, man, and that scares you. You really want to quit on her when she's pregnant with your son?"

"No way," Angello shakes his head. "She'd have told me."

"You are a dumb grunt. Shaila wants you in her life because you want to take a risk on love, not out of some misguided sense of duty. I'll never hold my baby girl. Hell, I've never even looked into her eyes except from this in-between place. But, that isn't the plan the Commander-in-Chief has for me."

"So, you've, uh, got orders . . . from God?"

"That's need-to-know information and right now, you don't need to know. Just remember this: every choice you make doesn't just affect only you."

Mike leans in close to Angello like a drill instructor bearing down on a new recruit.

"Don't screw this up. I'm counting on you."

Angello feels his stomach lurch the way it does when a chopper dives into a spin. And he is spiraling down, down, down in darkness. Until he stops, suspended above his own body shrouded in a snowy sheath.

ANGELLO GASPS FOR AIR. Feels an electrifying jolt as his soul reenters his body. Bright light shines in his face.

A shadow moves over him.

"Hey buddy, can you hear me?" It's a man's voice.

"Where am I?" Angello feels movement beneath him.

"We're wheeling you into Trinity Medical Center ER. I'm Joe, an EMT," he says. "You're lucky we happened to be on the way back from another call. We nearly ran over the half of your bike that was lying in the middle of the road. What's your name?"

"Angello. There was . . . someone with me."

"Someone was riding with you? We didn't find anyone else," Joe tells him.

"No. Someone . . . just out there."

"Buddy, the only other thing out there is eight inches of snow and another foot on the way. Freak Nor'easter."

JOE STOPS THE GURNEY at the nurse's station and gives her Angello's vitals: alert and responsive. Concussion likely. Needs neuro and ortho eval. The nurse directs Joe to a curtained exam room where Angello is hooked up to various monitors. She informs Angello a doctor will be with him as soon as possible. She hands him the buzzer, then leaves the room. Before Joe follows her out, he turns to Angello.

"On second thought, there was something kind of strange out there," Joe says. "An owl perched right on the back of our emergency vehicle. Kept hooting at us as we brought you up from the embankment."

As Joe leaves, a woman pushes past him. Snowflakes shimmer in her long, chestnut hair. Mascara streaks her cheeks.

"Angello!"

"Shaila!" Angello coughs. "What are you doing here?"

She sits on a chair next to the bed. Her petite hand, just out of a white mitten, feels warm against his cold, clammy skin. He weaves his long fingers between hers.

He remembers; she's listed as next of kin.

She rolls her lips in that funny way Angello learned long ago to recognize when she felt uncertain. She glances down at their hands before gently pulling hers back into her lap and sitting back against the chair.

Aware of the space she's just put between them, Angello raises the bed and lets out a pained grunt. He buzzes the nurse to ask for medication.

"You missed your flight because of me."

"No." She draws in a deep breath and sighs.

"It was the storm. I got a text on my way to the airport. The flight was canceled. I wasn't far from the hospital when they called about your accident."

"Why were you even on the road?" She pauses and looks out the window at the falling snow. She blinks back the tears that fill her eyes. "Maybe I don't want to know."

The nurse and a doctor arrive; the nurse scolds Angello for raising the bed. Shaila stands up and steps to the end of the bed, out of their way. The nurse administers pain meds through Angello's IV, then directs Shaila to the waiting room.

"Shaila, wait. I want . . . ask you something . . ."

Light shining in his eyes. Angello's mind flashes back to the woods. The owl. Mike.

And he drifts off into darkness, again.

A RUSH OF AIR TICKLES the nape of his neck. The owl flies over Angello's head and perches in a barren tree ahead, in the dark. Those amber eyes look down at him and the owl hoots softly as if to say, "Follow me." Golden light rises up with the mist, revealing a path beyond the trees. The owl swoops down and flies over Angello again. It looks back mid-flight and hoots. Mesmerized by the light and now by the owl's call, Angello begins to follow.

The light along the path is warm, comforting . . . freeing. Ahead, familiar silhouettes appear. He cannot see faces yet Angello knows these are his brothers. They are waiting for him. The owl soars ahead toward the figures, and then back to Angello, encouraging him to move forward. He is willing, ready to stop fighting the owl.

Just a few more steps and he'll reach his brothers . . . but, there's a faint calling of his name from somewhere behind him. He turns to look. There she is: Shaila, at his bedside, praying over him. Talking to him. He is pulled equally toward her and to the light. The owl perches on a tree above him, in this space on the path between life and death. And he remembers Mike's words to him, "Every choice you make doesn't just affect you."

Angello turns and begins walking . . . not toward the light but away from it. He turns his head to look back at the silhouettes. A few put up their hands and wave him off. The owl calls. Angello makes the hardest choice yet, but for once in a long time the right choice.

Last

Gerry Huntman

Gerry Huntman is a writer and publisher based in Australia. He has sold over 50 short fiction pieces to the market in Australia, the United States, and the UK. He has also published a middle grade fantasy novel, *Guardian of the Sky Realms*, through Meerkat Press (with a contracted sequel forthcoming). He lives in the hinterlands of the Gold Coast with his wife and teenage daughter. "Last" first appeared in *Planet Magazine*.

HE DIDN'T REMEMBER his name, but he was sure he once had one. It disturbed him that his memory was faulty and his thinking was so unclear. He could smell burning wire, which indicated internal damage—this caused him to react quickly, as his life depended on swift action.

He picked himself up from the twisted metal and churned earth that he lay in and stumbled up a small mound—the motors that assisted his movement were laboring, which was a bad sign. He wasn't well coordinated, and he felt as if his nervous system had been damaged in some way; an uneasy feeling crept through his being—it was starting to look like he may have suffered brain damage.

On the top of the mound he stood up and looked about the terrain of the world that he was in. The servo-mechanisms that supported the telescopic vision in his helmet whined and strained, but it eventually succeeded in allowing him a wide field of vision. Utter devastation. A landscape cracked with spewing magma and mountains that had spilled over plains. A large metal city was ruined, broken, and steaming as if it had ancient fires that had never been extinguished. The atmosphere was devoid of breathable air and he was glad that his armored suit was still feeding him oxygen and protecting him from the extreme heat.

His vision blurred for a few disorienting seconds, and his right leg twitched, nearly causing him to fall. He heard electricity arcing in his chest and noticed a readout from his HUD that indicated that backup systems were mounting. He was gravely concerned that if he didn't find technicians and medics soon, he would die.

The thought of finding a rescuer was an excellent thread of thinking—he needed to contact others; anyone. He opened all communication channels and sent a distress signal. In the meantime, he opened all receiver channels and got nothing . . . not a single intelligible radio signal, no digital data at all. His communication systems were sophisticated enough to determine that not one mechanism was transmitting on the entire planet. The lack of response to his distress comms troubled him. It appeared that an entire planet's civilization had been destroyed. It was likely the planet was lifeless. Except for him.

"I am the last."

He wanted to cry but he couldn't. It seemed strange, but he guessed that the brain damage was more extensive than what he first thought. There was a numbness in his thinking, and the world had a haziness about it that he had not experienced before; almost as if it was unreal. He wondered what he could do next, but the problem was that as long as his memory and senses were so impaired, he had very little information to work with. He looked to the ruined city again and tried one more time to use all of his equipment to find some possibility of life—infrared broad-spectrum filters, motion-pattern sensing beams, nano-level organo-chemical sensors, and another attempt at end-to-end communication frequencies.

To no avail.

"I am the last."

He realized that there was little point continuing his search for life or refuge unless he could find out more about his own situation. He shut down external based systems and turned on internal diagnostics. There was damage in the relay circuitry, and it took a long time to redirect the digital path for information to return to him. Wires arced and he nearly lost his footing again.

First layer reporting finally appeared on his console, indicating that most of his superstructure had been damaged in one form or another—his armor was riddled with holes and rents, and eighteen reinforcement struts were snapped. He was utterly confused. How can this be and yet I am still alive?

Second layer reporting provided metrics that indicated that a quarter of the armor's electronic systems and sensors were impaired. This made sense.

Third layer reporting validated that all memory storage was intact. Again, it didn't make sense to him. Why can't I remember anything?

Fourth layer reporting established that the human in the armored suit was lifeless, and had been deceased for three years, four months, twenty-seven days, eight hours and seventeen minutes . . . He paused. He was more baffled than ever.

He couldn't work out why he was thinking, searching, suffering, and yet his system was saying that he was dead. He wanted to panic, to scream out to the deaf world that he was alive, but again, his numbness, his damaged condition left him subdued.

The fifth and last layer report dribbled in its findings. It stated that the augmented AI system, which supported human tactical decision-making, control systems, and servo-mechanisms, was seriously impaired, but functional, but was at risk due to fuel cell leakage.

He was concerned with this last report, but hoped that he could contact the AI so that they could work together to repair his life support system. He tried every trick in the book to find digital paths to the other "brain" in the armored suit, but at every turn there was nothing. Nothing.

"I am the last."

He concluded that the diagnostics system must be faulty, which was the only logical reason why he was still alive, but had reluctantly accepted the fact that the AI was not contactable to provide him with assistance. He was still in the dark; confused.

He heard more arcing in his electronics and his left leg gave way, causing him to crash to the ground. He switched back to external functionality. His thinking started to blur again and . . . he saw a large tear in his titanium alloy arm and a human radius and ulna poking out, shrink-wrapped in dried flesh and skin.

As the fuel cell finally died, he realized his fundamental error, and wondered if dying was the same for him as it was for a human.

"I am the last . . ."

The Imidor

D. L. SHIREY

D. L. Shirey writes from Portland, Oregon, where it's usually raining. So he's usually writing. His short stories and non-fiction appear in 70 publications, with those flavored by science fiction featured in *Riggwelter*, *Theme of Absence*, *ZeroFlash*, and *365 Tomorrows*. You can find more of his writing at www.dlshirey.com and @dlshirey on X. "The Imidor" is original to *Bullet Points*.

BAZZY SITS ON THE PORCH STEPS of a farmhouse, sipping tea from the plastic cup that tops his Thermos. He is a large man, chubbier than any of the locals. His mess of hair and four-day beard are black. His eyes match the dark gray bandana tied loosely around his neck. Today is his forty-first birthday, although he is far away from anyone who would care enough to celebrate.

Bazzy carries his tea things with him in a camo shoulder bag. The bag and uniform make locals assume Bazzy is military. He is not, although there is a small army of people like Bazzy dispatched to the region on similar assignments. They call themselves Imidors, even though their proper designation is United Nations Data Corps.

"More?" The woman on the other side of the screen door holds a saucepan with steaming water.

"I've had enough tea, thanks."

"For your Thermos then." She has a kind voice.

"It's already full. I can use the water to shave, if you don't mind."

"Of course." She opens the door and sets the pot on the porch. As she bends, the woman flattens her palm against her breastbone, pressing the dingy fabric of her dress tight against her crepey skin. Bazzy rolls his eyes at the woman's modesty. There's no thrill in sneaking a peek at the old widow's breasts.

Bazzy stands and stretches his back. The last swallow of tea is tepid and delicious. Rangdoo Darjeeling tastes better as it cools, even when born of barbaric brewing accoutrements and sipped from a plastic cup. A battlefield is no place for porcelain or tea ceremonies. He uses his bandana to swab out specks of tea leaves from the camp-fire coffee pot, then packs it with the strainer, infuser, and tins of tea.

Bazzy withdraws a shaving kit from his bag, setting each item side by side on the porch rail. He fetches the pan of hot water, then dips his shaving brush and swirls the bristles against a bar of soap; he does this a second and third time until the brush is lathered. Bazzy sweeps soap on his beard, using a palm-sized mirror to check coverage.

He reaches for the bandana and, before he wipes his hands, studies it. "Have you a clean rag?" he shouts at the house, then inches the straight razor down cheek, chin, and neck, examining each clean patch in the mirror.

The woman returns and drapes an embroidered hand towel across his shoulder.

"Keep it," she says.

Bazzy tilts the mirror in her direction and gives her a wink. She returns a weary smile. If she was beautiful once, it's impossible to tell now.

AS SOON AS HE FINISHES shaving, his tactical smartwatch vibrates with text coordinates. Tapping the link activates the GPS and topo map designating Bazzy's search grid. He repacks his belongings with the neatly folded towel on top. Shouldering the bag, he waves goodbye, assuming the woman is watching from the house.

The search site is south-southeast. Bazzy can walk along a road to get there, always preferable than a cross-country trek with God-knows-what kind of terrain or impediment. Land mines were out-lawed several wars ago, but some of those suckers were made of plastic, designed to be undetectable, and built to last. Even thirty years later.

This road is no walk in the park. Monoliths of asphalt rut up from too many heavy vehicles, the shoulders heaped with litter and junk. Bazzy inserts earbuds. Music will help while away the hours, but the primary purpose is to listen for IMIDs. Anything active within twenty meters will sound a chime.

He hears angelic sopranos sing *Lakmé's* "Flower Duet" and all five movements of *Grand Canyon Suite* before a chime interrupts a pianist plowing through Rachmaninov. His watch automatically switches to detection mode; it points right, off-road, twelve meters. Bazzy reaches over his shoulder and unhooks the carabiner holding his walking stick. He telescopes the aluminum tubes to full length and wraps the leather thong around his wrist. He unsnaps the sheath holding his Buck knife.

Just over a rise is a single, conical crater. Bazzy shakes his head. "Maneater," he says aloud. After four years Bazzy can diagnose which weaponry was used just from the blast hole.

Maneater missiles are a more recent addition to military arsenals, usually used by underfinanced armies that scavenge a battlefield to resupply their soldiers. Maneaters vaporize any animal: people, livestock, rodents, birds, and insects. Plus leather, wool, bone, feathers, or anything made from animal byproducts. Maneaters spare all equipment, weapons, ammunition, and the rest of the stuff. Including IMIDs.

What remains of animals reminds Bazzy of the brittle, golden shell that tops crème brûlée. It cracks when walked on, and coats everything in the vicinity of the former creature in weird Rorschach-like patterns. Bazzy can determine the relative size of the beast from the residue, but not a rabbit from a crow, nor a human from a goat. Since this area has already been picked clean by scavengers, most clues that can identify a soldier are gone. All personal effects have been plundered. Jewelry, obviously, but everything else as well, from prosthetics to zippers.

Bazzy tries to tiptoe around the brûlée, often an impossible task. His walking stick cracks open one of the brittle pools and Bazzy spies a square of white. He unsheaths his Buck knife and flips over a crystalline shard. There, underneath, are the contents of a vaporized wallet, the plastic cards and papers still stacked and folded as if the leather was still there. Next to it is an IMID.

This one was hidden from view, but, as Bazzy stands, he can see a few of the bright yellow, aspirin-sized discs scattered about.

Those who scavenge battlefields know to leave IMIDs behind. Their countrymen may be among the dead, and the UNDC's casualty report is the only way to find out for sure.

Bazzy doesn't touch anything just yet but keeps walking to the far edge of the Maneater's blast radius. His detector counts seventeen in the area and begins compiling a list of their owners. One by one, each implant IDs a soldier's name, rank, serial number, date, and place of birth. More data can be gleaned once the IMIDs are collected, processed, and returned to the country of origin.

Bazzy sighs and slips the Thermos from his bag's side pocket. He wishes there was another cup of tea inside, but the contents rattle as he unscrews the top. He picks up one yellow disc after another, dropping them in with the others.

"Happy birthday to me," he says aloud, happy, for the moment. No corpses means he doesn't have to extract IMIDs from decomposing bodies.

Autumn Corn

TYREE CAMPBELL

> Tyree Campbell is a retired U.S. Army translator
> with several novels, novellas, and short stories
> published. He also writes the *Bombay Sapphire*
> superheroine series for Pro Se Press. He lives in the
> Southwest with two husky mixes who keep him in
> shape. "Autumn Corn" originally appeared in
> *History Through Fiction*.

THE EVENING BEFORE THE INVADERS reached Earth, several of us who had nothing else to do chose to await the inevitable outcome inside Twohy's, one of those increasingly rare and stubborn establishments that still served the full-flavored imported brands of alcohol and tobacco. Every few minutes, curt nods and desultory waves of greeting indicated the arrival of yet another regular, and when the counter population began to approach capacity I repaired to a dimly-lit corner booth with a full mug of English winter ale to watch and listen.

For the most part, the regulars sat quietly, nursing drinks and feeding from the canisters of bar nuts. Now and then two heads leaned closer together in the dull blue haze to share some anecdote, then separated once more to brood over private thoughts, concerns, anxieties. In that respect, the evening differed not a whit from any of the other thousand or so I'd passed in Twohy's during the decade I'd been a city beat news contributor.

Interspersed among the gathering I spotted several unfamiliar faces—despite the high cost of electricity, Padraig Twohy kept the outside lights on at night so that anyone who sought a nocturnal refuge would know he or she was welcome here, and on this chilly night in late autumn more than a few had accepted the invitation. Soon the coat rack was overburdened, and Padraig sent one of his serving girls round to gather up the excess and deposit it neatly—with the owners' consent—in one of the back storage rooms. My own overcoat was draped over the end of the partition between my booth and the adjoining unit. It blocked my view of the newcomer until he was standing beside the empty bench opposite me.

"Mind if I sit meself down?" he asked, the head of his ale spilling down the side of his mug. "The other booths be full, a'most, and I was thinking . . ."

At first, in the poor lighting, I thought him a bag man, so scruffy he was, but as I took in the whole of his tattered attire I realized that the look was cultivated, deliberate. A row of military medals across his left breast lent credence to his uniform, as it were—a uniform of disparate fragments from Goodwill and Salvation Army.

Despite his condition, he smelled pleasantly of lavender, grass, and something vaguely metallic, almost like blood. I bade him sit down, and he did, as if he were older than time itself. My overcoat trembled with his impact. Following a casual toast in my direction he took a long pull from his ale, then placed the mug carefully on the table and curled protective fingers around it. For a few seconds he glanced out the window, as if looking for something in the night. The eyes of his reflection met mine.

Finally he smiled, and extended a rough, calloused hand. "John Towton," he announced. He sounded not quite English; Canadian, perhaps. I introduced myself as Colin Hastings, omitting the "Chug" by which the Twohy's regulars addressed me. "A name from the Old Country," said Towton.

"I was born and raised right here in Chicago," I said. Light from the overhead panels fell on his shirt, and I briefly inspected his medals, recognizing none of them. "Which war were you in?" I inquired.

Towton took another pull of ale, then gazed speculatively at his mug, and through it into Time itself. "All of them," he whispered.

Unbidden, one of Twohy's serving girls brought me a fresh ale and, so help me, curtseyed, the neckline of her cream and gold frock opening to reveal the upper swells of her bosom. It was impossible for me not to notice, because I had been looking in the general direction of the mug when she dipped. Belatedly I realized that Towton was staring at her in frank admiration. Then, quite abruptly, he blinked and pulled himself back from his notions, and from her departure. His bushy, gray-black eyebrows knotted as if at some memory that was refusing his active recollection.

"Time was," he whispered.

There were laws nobody bothered to enforce these days, including the establishment of temporary liaisons, ones against underage employment in drinking establishments. I said, "Nicole is all of nineteen."

"Aye, hard it's been to keep up with the changes." Towton lifted his mug again, and his voice took on a heavy accent. "T'yer 'ealth."

"Changes," I said, but Towton did not elaborate. Again he gazed through the window, searching for something in the night the way a shaman scans entrails, to find meaning in the glass-distorted darkness. Suddenly he shivered, as if a chill wind had blown in, though the air inside Twohy's was warm and still and hazy, and in that moment the lights began to flicker again, as if yet another outage were imminent.

"I hear the foe advancing," Towton said softly, to the window.

The way he said it felt oddly familiar, its point of reference maddeningly elusive. A martial song, perhaps. "They'll arrive just after dawn," I reminded him. "That's the schedule the Invaders announced when they issued the ultimatum to the UN." I sighed. "We should have negotiated."

Towton smiled at me, tolerant of an ingenuous child. In his left eye, pale in the tavern light, pooled a single tear. With the effort he made to hold it back, his face took on the façade of a defeated yet unbowed general. "Just once," he said. "I want to win just once."

"In all those wars you mentioned," I said, still skeptical, "you chose the losing side?"

Towton's barked laugh made heads turn momentarily, but where the others might have detected astonished mirth, I, who had a clear view of his face, heard only an ancient bitterness, and I knew that for reasons I did not yet fathom, choice had been denied him.

"Tell me," I said.

Towton considered the request briefly, then shook his head. "There is too much to tell."

But what was time or money to me, to any of us, now? "I'll supply the ale to keep your voice lubricated," I said—a lesson I had learned as a young war correspondent. The offer seemed to sway Towton, and I signaled to Nicole. After she brought fresh lubrication, Towton drank half of his. The ale affected neither his equilibrium nor his voice.

"Who knows how far into the mists of Time it begins," he said. Once more the lights flickered briefly, and I lit a small tapered candle. Towton frowned his disapproval at the overhead lights, as if they were somehow under his control. "They came because they were takers," he went on, in a voice with the substance of echoes inside an ancient tunnel. "Ever taking more, until they came to a land happy and empty, though it were inhabited by folk far older than they. They took lands not theirs, and built their walls upon them, disturbed the glens and the forests. Outraged the queen and her daughters. For a while we fought successfully, putting myriads of them to axe and fire. But our emotion spent itself, and they were trained for slaughter. On Watling Street we did die—I myself fell upon a glen to the Fourteenth Legion—and it was over, over," and here Towton idly rubbed the left side of his chest, just above the row of medals, and took another swallow of ale. "The language did not survive, nor the folkways. Gone, all gone."

His voice trailed off, while I found nothing to say. He looked old and decrepit enough actually to have fought in the battles of which he spoke, and that was impossible, of course. Still, there was something in his eyes, ancient as night, that fixed me to his words, his story, and most of all to his haunted, desolate tone—the tone of one who could be killed, but not defeated.

Nicole's elbow jostled me as she reached across the table for Towton's hand. I did not recall her having joined us. Young she might be, but in that moment she became every-soldier's woman.

"That is one battle," I said, after a moment.

With a visible effort Towton drew his eyes from the young woman and fixed me with the sorrow in them. "All my battles are alike, sir. What one folk possess, another, mightier, may claim. I crawled alongside Vercingetorix when they dragged him to Rome. I walked the Trail of Tears to Sand Creek. I was Etruscan until the advent of the Romans, a Visigoth before the Moors flooded Spain. I died on the walls of Harlech, a thousand times have I seen my comrades and my kinfolk scythed down like autumn corn . . .

"Now my people live on reservations, the Celtic language is as dead as Gaul, the Carthaginians are known only to history, Etruscan is found appropriately on markers in ancient cemeteries, the Visig-oths might as well have never existed. Who now marks the changing of the seasons and the stars, who foretells the coming winter by the actions of the wee creatures, who plants . . .

"And how many more, sir, how many more peoples and folk are gone, vanished, because they were technologically inferior, unable to cope with the onslaughts of others who sought their lands, their resources, their space? How many folkways have been ground to dust? All gone, gone. All my battles have been lost, and lost 'ere they were even begun."

Haggard and torn was Towton, but behind the sorrow in his eyes was not a trace of surrender. "And yet, you fight on," I said.

"Like Cyrano at the last, against his old enemies."

He turned baleful eyes toward me, and I knew what he was going to ask, and I felt hollow, as if my heart were pumping but no blood would course. Upon my shoulders settled the weight of all those who had been beaten, whatever their cause. Some hoped to survive by trying to get along and going with the flow; others were doomed by their consciences to oppose, whatever the cost.

"And you, sir," said Towton. "Will you not fight?"

I wanted to protest that I was a reporter, an observer. I watched what went on, and told of it. That was my lot in life. I even opened my mouth to say as much.

"No," said Towton. "I see that you will not." He raised his voice, eyes sweeping the tavern. "Will any man here fight alongside me? Any one of you, will ye fight along with me?"

A silence fell upon the room, brief yet eternal. No man looked at Towton. It was as if some minor unexpected event had occurred, and everyone had paused, thinking, "Huh? What?" But Towton's invitation held no context for them, no referent; it was too mad to be possible. A moment later, it had never happened, and the quiet hum of gathered people resumed.

Towton was looking at Nicole again, with eyes only for her, his knuckled and calloused right hand captured by her petite two. "My dear, I am but an old soldier, about to do battle one more time. Where can we go?"

"There is a utility closet, sir."

And nothing more was said between them. I watched them wind through the crowd of patrons, and pondered a report from the front lines that I would never write. The lights flickered and finally died, and candles soon added their smoke to the cigarettes and the cigars and the alcoholic mist. Towton might have appreciated this atmosphere of a medieval cellar, but I never saw him again.

Presently Nicole resumed her duties, a little color to her cheeks. Outside the window, flashes of light revealed purple-gray clouds just before dawn, and were extinguished. Nearby, a solitary incandescence lived and faded and died, and my heart weighed with Towton's latest death. There was nothing left for me to do except finish the ale, and wonder whether I would be one of the unfortunate few who lived long enough to learn the new language.

The Shauns

KELLEE KRANENDONK

Kellee Kranendonk has spent a lifetime writing. According to her late grandfather she was born with a pen in one hand and paper in the other. She's certain that these days he would have claimed she was born clutching a laptop. She's had over a hundred published stories, poems, and non-fiction pieces. Her work has received an honorable mention, she's been a spotlight author, and some of her pieces were to appear in a school book project, though that didn't pan out. Kellee has been an editor, has managed online writing groups, and one of her stories appeared in a best-selling anthology. She lives in a brand-new merged municipality in New Brunswick, Canada. "The Shauns" originally appeared in *The Martian Wave*.

I DON'T REALLY KNOW who I am.

I don't remember much before the beach incident—which is, I think, what started everything—except Shaun asking Della to marry him. And even that is a blur. I don't know if they adopted me or got married first or if it all happened at the same time. The memories blend together in my mind, their edges blurred, and mixed with things that don't make sense. Sometimes it feels like I woke up yesterday the newly adopted child of newlyweds, but mostly it seems like I've known Shaun and Della since before I existed.

Shaun and Della are my parents. Except I'm not really from their world. I know because they've told me I'm adopted. And because

I see things different from others. Things like storm clouds before they've even drifted to our little piece of sky or the color of a person's eyes while they're still several meters away.

Anyway, the beach thing. I remember Shaun and Della being all kissy-face with each other, so I started out on my own. I didn't know anybody so I wasn't looking for anyone in particular, just wanted to be alone with my thoughts. I wondered if this kissing thing was a custom on this world. Shouldn't I know something like that? Frustration grew as I tried to sort out my life beyond the beach, beyond the now.

I loved living here: the warm weather, the hot sand between my toes, the crash of the waves and cries of the gulls. This place seemed like paradise making me feel like I'd been here all my life. Yet something was missing. I longed for . . . what? The love of a parent? A mate? I glanced back at Shaun and Della. I knew they cared for me but at the same time I couldn't remember what they'd done to make me know that. And I was a kid, not ready for a mate yet, at least by human standards. Would I be all grown up on my home planet, with a mate and kids of my own?

Maybe that was it. Maybe I was missing my real home. Something sparked deep within me yet my memories shared no secrets. How could I desire something I couldn't remember?

There was a small grassy hill that overlooked the beach. I climbed it and sat looking out at the water, the sky, feeling the wind in my hair and on my skin. After a while I laid on my back and stared at the puffy white clouds, soaking in warmth from the beach sand and grass. Then I fell asleep.

When I awoke, my mouth was gritty with sand. Sitting up I tried working up some saliva to spit with. That's when I noticed the funnel clouds. Nobody on the beach seemed aware of them—they kept splashing and playing—but I knew I could see what they couldn't. They might have seen the darkening sky but not the elongated clouds that stretched down, touching the water. Even though I'd never seen anything like them before, I somehow knew those clouds were danger. I had to find Shaun and Della.

I jumped up, quickly brushed sand away from my tank top and shorts, then ran down the hill to the beach. I couldn't see them. Panic struck! Where had they gone? I started screaming Shaun's name and suddenly I couldn't move. Then I saw Della's bright orange top, just a small dot in the distance. I yelled her name but she didn't hear me.

I screamed for Shaun again but they weren't listening, and fear held me frozen.

Except it wasn't fear. After a few seconds I realized some guy had a hold of my clothes. Refusing to freak out, I asked him to let go.

"You were screaming for Shaun. Well, you got him," he said, grinning.

"Wrong Shaun," I said and tried pulling out of his grasp.

He hung on.

I glanced at the advancing dark clouds. I couldn't bear to lose Shaun and Della. I don't know why but the terror of losing them consumed me. I pulled against the Wrong Shaun. He just laughed and hung on.

Then I knelt. "You wanna play your way?"

He shrugged like this was some kind of game. I grabbed a handful of sand and threw it in his face. As he howled and clawed at his eyes, I ran for my parents.

"Shaun!"

He finally turned away from Della and got to his feet. "Tori, what is it?"

He put his hands on my shoulders, warm comfort against my skin, and looked into my eyes. I saw his concern but I saw confusion too and something I couldn't read. Guilt? I didn't care about whatever he and Della wanted to do, as long as they didn't abandon me. I told him about the clouds. He looked where I pointed but he couldn't see them even though they were as clear to me as my own fingers.

Della joined him. "We should probably listen to her." Her voice defied the fear in her eyes.

Then, somebody with a bluetooth speaker shouted. "Tornado. They're saying tornadoes are coming this way."

Shaun and Della looked at one another and nodded.

"I'll get Tori inside," said Shaun. "You—" He glanced at me then back to Della. "Get whoever you can."

I followed Shaun to the basement of our beach house, not really understanding what was going on, just that danger was on its way and my parents were trying to help whoever they could.

"Stay here," Shaun commanded, starting to leave.

"No." The panic started to rise again. "You have to stay. I came back for you, to keep you safe."

"Tori—"

"Please . . . daddy?"

"I'm sorry, Tori. I can't explain right now. But I promise I'll come back. I won't leave you." He turned to leave.

I grabbed his arm. "Then if you're going, you have to bring back the other Shaun."

"What other Shaun?"

"I threw sand at him. He couldn't see. You have to help him."

Shaun frowned. "Tori, I doubt—" He broke off, looking like he wanted to say something. But there was no time to explain, no time to sort out anything I was feeling. He ran off leaving me in our giant basement, alone until Della came in leading a long line of people. Kids held their parents' hands, teens walked arm in arm. I watched her settle them, admiring her, loving her. She was strong, a leader.

I knew she could make it on her own. But Shaun was still out there, struggling against whatever was happening. I wanted, maybe even needed, to help. I ran to the door.

"Tori, you can't leave." Della's voice was strong, authoritative.

I obeyed her, staying in the doorway, craning to see Shaun, eyeing the long black clouds winding their way closer.

Finally Shaun came back with the Wrong Shaun who kept blinking and squinting. I wanted to say I was sorry, but I wasn't. It was his own fault. He deserved to be saved, but not apologized to. He glared at me as they passed. A few stragglers followed the Shauns.

By now even the humans could see the black swirling funnel clouds with bursts of energy flashing inside. Wind blew down the basement stairs carrying grains of sand that stung as I tried pulling the door closed.

Shaun took the knob, brushing my hand away. He was strong enough to pull it closed. He smiled at me. "I promised you I'd come back."

I smiled back. But smiling wasn't what I was doing on the inside. "What's going on?" The wind outside howled as if in response to my inner turmoil.

"It'll be okay here," Shaun assured me. "We have to get everybody to the inner rooms."

I looked around. Everyone, even the other Shaun, was gone.

"Della's already done that."

She popped her head around the corner. "Are you two coming?"

"Let's go," said Shaun.

OUR BASEMENT, like the house above it, was so large you could almost get lost. There was an outer hallway that circled around several smaller, inner rooms. Shaun and I made one circle around, to make sure no one was left behind, before joining Della and the others.

The inner rooms had brick walls painted to look as though they had windows. But it made no difference to the people here. Kids cried, adults complained, and teenagers looked bored. Or scared. Sometimes both.

The house shook a couple of times and I could see the distress in Shaun's and Della's eyes that no one else could, as they mingled with the others, always coming back to one corner for a few moments before mingling again.

As I watched them standing together, whispering to one another, I wondered if they were discussing the storm, maybe talking about me or sharing little love secrets. Then I noticed the Wrong Shaun. He stood in a doorway staring at me. I turned away but I could still feel his eyes boring into my back. Why had he grabbed me?

I tried walking among the people, getting lost in their numbers, but no one wanted to talk to me.

They were worried about this thing they called a tornado. Some of them were checking their devices, and the guy with the bluetooth speaker was hooking the device up to his phone. Probably looking for news on an FM station.

I finally found a place to lean against a wall where I was close to them, but away from the Wrong Shaun's eyes. Sliding down the wall, I put my head on my knees. Even though I looked human, I wasn't, and I didn't like this any more than they did. A hundred thoughts ran through my head: What was a tornado and how dangerous was it really? What about all the other people still out there? Where did I really come from? Why was I here? What did the Wrong Shaun want from me?

A clear image formed in my mind among the confusion. A man with short black hair, at least I think it was a man. I couldn't see his face or body clearly. Except for his hand. He held a knife. No, a . . . a stick? He jabbed it towards me. Pressed it against my temple. He wanted to kill me! Panic! I had to get away from him. Pain exploded in my head.

"Shaun!" I lifted my head. People were looking at me. Shaun and Della were looking at me. I felt my face flush as I got to my feet. I hadn't cried out on purpose. Moving toward my parents, I once again saw the Wrong Shaun watching me. He looked as if he was waiting for something. But what? For me to make some kind of stupid mistake? For me to decide that I liked him after all?

"Daddy," I whimpered, entering the safe circle of Shaun's arms. If anyone could make another feel safe, it was a father.

"It's time, Shaun," said Della, looking at the thing on her wrist that she called a watch. "We can't wait anymore. Tori!" She spat out my name as if I were her servant.

Shaun took his arms from around me and turned to her. "Della?"

Her face hardened for a moment, as if she was angry with him. I slid my hand around his arm. I felt the need to protect him, but I didn't know why. Surely these two had had arguments before. Then her face softened and she looked at me.

"I need your help, Tori. Are you okay with that?"

I nodded. I could do anything for her as long as I could get past the Wrong Shaun.

"First I need you to carefully check to see if the . . ."

"Della, we can't send her out there. I can check."

Della laughed. "I know daddy wants to protect his little girl. But she'll be fine. I need you with me." She slipped her hand around his other arm and pulled him over to her side. Then she looked at me. "I need you to see if the tornadoes are over. Look out a window on the beach side and let me know what you see." She stressed the word "tornadoes" as if that's not what they really were.

"Okay. I can do this, Dad. It's okay."

As I headed for the door, another image flashed through my mind. Long, black funnel clouds reaching down from the sky, dropping here, there, probing, looking for . . . It was gone, leaving me more confused. Were tornadoes weather systems or alien life-forms?

The Wrong Shaun matched my movements as I continued across the room. Cursing myself for feeling pity and asking for him to be brought to safety, I swallowed my fear until he grabbed my arm. "Don't do this."

Panic I couldn't control swarmed me again like a hungry beast that lived inside me, never to be fed. "Please don't."

With his other hand he grabbed my chin and turned my face to look at him. His fingers caressed my face, his dark eyes bored into mine but I refused to look away. He pleaded silently with me. But for what?

"Take your hands off my daughter."

I looked away to see Shaun approaching, anger on his face. Della was beside him but she looked more worried than angry.

"She's not—" started the Wrong Shaun but then he stopped and let go of me. "Do what you must," he growled.

"Stay away from her," hissed Della, pointing her finger at the Wrong Shaun. Then she pulled at my dad. "Come on. Why did you bring him in here?"

"Tori asked me—" The rest was lost in the buzz of the crowd

Out in the hall, on the beach side of the house, I carefully moved a gray and yellow floral curtain aside and peered out. The water churned, roiling as if greatly disturbed. Roaring wind blew sand against the window and the long black clouds moved erratically about over both land and water, discharging bolts of electricity. These were the tornadoes I'd envisioned, but what were they doing?

There was a loud snap and the house shuddered. Somehow I knew we'd been hit. I dropped the curtain and ran back to the inner rooms to tell Shaun. His face scrunched in fear and confusion. But before he could say anything, Della spoke.

"I told you, Shaun. We have to do this now."

"What about all these people?"

She shrugged and shook her head.

Shaun grabbed my hand. "Come with me, Tori."

He led me through the maze of halls and rooms, some empty, some furnished and others with boxes piled haphazardly around. We arrived in a small room, just big enough for the two of us, and possibly a third person. To the left sat a chair, encircled by panels and controls. I looked at him.

"What is this?"

"You know what this is." His voice had changed. Rough and hard, it was no longer the soothing daddy voice I knew.

"No." I shook my head, but even as I did I realized it all looked familiar somehow.

"Just sit and do what you have to do." He nudged me toward the chair.

I sat, barely aware of his voice and actions. The buttons and controls were like an old familiar map to me. I still didn't know who I really was, but I knew these panels. I knew how to make this ship run. I reached for a panel and . . . Ship?

I looked at Shaun. He stood there watching me, his back to the door. His face safe and comforting, yet his voice belied that. I looked at the panels again, this time pressing buttons, pushing levers, keying and locking in coordinates. A smooth hum and a soft shake began. I sat back, pleased with what I'd done. Once more I looked at Shaun. This time for answers. "What have I done?"

He smiled. Then the color drained from his face and he dropped to the floor. Behind him stood the Wrong Shaun.

"You remember now," he said.

I shook my head. "I only remembered how to work these controls." I noticed the panic didn't rise. I looked at Shaun and wondered if he was dead. I went to him.

"He's stunned, not dead," said the Wrong Shaun. "Do you still think he's your father?"

"Who else would he be? What did you do to him? Does he need a doctor?"

"Torrencia."

It was a simple enough word. My name, actually. My real name. My life before Shaun and Della on the beach raced through my mind in the seconds it took me to look from the man who claimed to be my father to the other Shaun.

A long time ago, my people—the Lirs—had left a dying world on a ship. Dying because of a war—fought between my people and those of the Shauns. His name wasn't Shaun, he was a Shaun.

I had been on that ship. I had, in fact, captained it. But when we entered Earth's atmosphere, many Lir had died—mostly the very old or the very young. I was a survivor, not someone's teenaged child.

I'd landed the ship on vacant land near the ocean. Prepared specifically for this venture, it looked enough like a human house so as not to be blatantly alien. And it blended in enough to hide us from the Shauns.

We'd had to make a choice—live among the humans or take a chance on the cryo-freezers that had been installed but never tested. The technology worked on tamed *hoygas*. Although we resembled humans, and could have blended in, we chose the cryogenics. *Hoyga* genetics were close to ours and the freezing would prevent the Shauns from detecting our presence, should they stumble upon the planet where we'd chosen to hide.

One Lir was chosen to stay awake, keep the freezers running, keep us safe. Compared to humans, Lir live an exceptionally long time so we had no fear of not seeing him again.

I looked into Shaun's eyes, stood up and backed away from the man on the ground, still not fully comprehending everything. He moved farther into the room so I had to turn to face him. He sighed, sadness in his eyes. "Still don't trust me?"

I wasn't sure. "Who are you? Who's he, and what exactly is going on?"

"All good questions." Della's voice came from the doorway behind me. Shaun's eyes went to her. I turned to see her holding a *takstaka* on me. A long and narrow weapon, it looked like a stick with a bump on the bottom. But aimed right, a single blast from it could blow away me and the Wrong Shaun at the same time. This morning I was her child. Now she was holding me at *takpoint.*

Della looked at the Wrong Shaun. "You should have left her alone."

"Wrong," he responded. "You should have left her."

He leapt at Della. She fired at him. I screamed as her blast hit his upper arm. The Shaun on the floor groaned. I kicked him as Della and the Wrong Shaun struggled. He managed to knock the *tak* out of her hands. It spun across the floor and landed out of Della's reach. I grabbed it and pointed it at her. "Questions need answers."

With two good arms, she grabbed the Wrong Shaun and thrust him in front of her, his right arm hanging useless at his side, cauterized by the *tak*, but shoulder dislocated.

"He's an acceptable loss," I claimed, though I wasn't sure he was. I vaguely felt that he could fill that void I'd felt this morning.

But Della believed me and let him go. He reached over and slapped something on the control panel. There was a slight lurch that I recognized as the ship stopping. "What are you doing?" I asked.

Della sneered. "Ivano did his job well."

What was she talking about? "Who?"

She pointed to the Shaun on the floor. "He erased your memory and filled your head with all kinds of human nonsense. Unfortunately, it seems he forgot to erase the trigger that would bring it all back, Torrencia."

More memories flooded back, mixed with emotion. The Wrong Shaun—his real name was Salax—was my husband. He'd been the one chosen to stay behind when the rest of us had been frozen. Because I was the captain, I had no choice but to get in the freezer. He worked as a chef—expendable. The hardest choice either of us had ever had to make. I choked back the urge to pull him into my arms. Instead I drove the end of the *tak* into Della's chest. "Answers."

She snorted. "Taking over your planet wasn't enough. We wanted to purge the universe of the Lir scum. We detected his blood—"

"She's lying," said Salax. "There's no way she could have detected the *ferrons* in my blood."

Ferron detection. I recalled the device the Shauns had. No Lir could ever hide from a Shaun with those devices. That had to be how they'd found us. But *ferrons* couldn't be detected when they were frozen, so how had it worked? I looked at Salax. He was the only way.

"I had no choice but to live among the humans," he explained. "I got a job as a chef, but one rainy night . . . I wasn't paying attention. There was an accident. I nearly died. I needed a blood transfusion. There wouldn't have been enough *ferrons* in my blood to detect.

"New and improved *ferron* detection," boasted Della. "And I figured it out. Even if you had 95 percent human blood, I could still detect the remaining 5 percent Lir blood."

No one said anything so I jabbed my weapon into Della's side to get her talking again. Obviously there was more to the story.

"After the war ended, Shauns were being tried for war crimes, so we ran. The ship Ivano and I were on crashed. We stumbled upon this place and I knew we could get back as long as we had you to fly this ship." She looked at me.

"She's still lying," mumbled Salax.

I tightened my grip on the trigger.

"Okay," she yelled. "We did crash. But I was the only survivor. I found the ship and the freezers and came up with a plan.

"I was the one who erased and replaced your memory." She paused, then sneered at me. "I didn't know there was a trigger word to bring it all back."

Salax grinned. "Her brain-training worked. Using a real name as a trigger instead of our common war names was how we defeated your memory-erasing technology."

Della sneered. "He must have still been in the hospital when I arrived. He wasn't part of the plan. I knew nothing about him until he showed up here."

Brain-trained. I remembered now. Torrencia Tua'dathan had captained that ship as Captain Tori Dathan. That was the name I'd given Della, or whoever she was. "So, who's Ivano?" I asked.

"My brother," said Salax. "And his name's not Ivano. It's Fralyn." He looked at me. "He loved you like a sister. He would have given his life for either one of us."

So, he wasn't even a Shaun after all.

I didn't need to hear more. The last dregs of memory had kicked in. The funnel clouds I'd seen were not tornadoes like the humans had thought. Nor were they aliens as I had considered. They were detectors, Lir looking for runaway Shauns, like Della and whoever had died in the crash.

I grabbed Salax's good arm and pulled him close to me. Then I aimed at Della and pulled the trigger.

AFTER CONTACTING THE SEARCH SHIP, setting Salax's shoulder, and making sure Fralyn was okay, I landed our ship and allowed the humans to go free. Della probably had plans to make them her slaves.

"Why did you knock out your own brother?" I asked Salax, as we watched the confused people milling about aimlessly on the beach, looking for signs of a storm, for the things they'd left behind. "And why couldn't he see the way I did? Don't all Lir see that way?"

"Yeah, Salax, why *did* you knock me out?"

"Della had him so confused he didn't know who he was," said Salax. "I was afraid he'd hurt you. And I have no idea why he couldn't see properly."

Fralyn shrugged. "I don't remember."

"Do you think Della was telling the truth?" I asked.

Salax shrugged. "She was running from something."

"There's only one way to find out," said Fralyn.

I smiled and closed the door. "I'll lift off. You guys go see if she left any more of us in the freezers."

I pushed buttons, tapped screens. Fralyn didn't have enough knowledge to pilot the ship. That was probably a good thing. Who knew what kind of trouble "Della" would have gotten us into? Though not trained as a pilot, Salax probably could have managed it. Since dear old "mom" was insistent on me flying, it seemed likely she was unaware of that. As egoistic as it might sound, I was the best choice.

No other pilot had flown this ship, and I had only ever piloted this one.

Fralyn started off. Salax leaned over to kiss me. I still loved him even though he was more human than Lir. But I couldn't help wondering how all of this had really changed us.

The Coldest Ride in the Dead of Winter

MIKE SHARLOW

Recently, Mike Sharlow moved from his hometown, a small city on the banks of the Mississippi, to a big city in the desert. He traded the subzero winter temperatures in the Midwest for the oven-hot summer in the Southwest. Sharlow has had over forty short story publications. His novel, *Welcome to the Ranks of the Enchanted*, is included in the Charvat Special American Fiction Collections at The Ohio State University. "The Coldest Ride in the Dead of Winter" originally appeared in *Purple Wall Stories*.

THE SNOWSTORM WAS FOLLOWED by a cold snap two days later. It was −3°F at 10:00 p.m., and with the windchill it felt like −15°F. I had a treacherous bike ride ahead of me, six miles round trip, on snow-covered roads.

When it was this cold, I had to layer up. From the waist down I wore long underwear, jeans, and gray sweatpants. On my upper body I had on a T-shirt, a flannel shirt, a hooded sweatshirt, and my insulated leather coat. On my head, I wore my winter face mask (only my eyes were exposed), a stocking cap, my sweatshirt hood, and my coat hood. I wore gloves thin enough so that I could slide my insulated leather mittens over them. I wore two pairs of socks and insulated hiking boots. My glasses protected my eyes from the wind.

I had to get in the right mindset to battle this frigid side of Mother Nature. At times like this she was challenging and cruel, and I hated her.

"Where's your gun?" I asked, my voice muffled from my face mask. Winnie picked up the AR-15 from the floor to show me then set it back down on the table in front of her without taking her eyes from her textbook. She was planning to be a doctor. Even though school wasn't in session, and it was likely it wouldn't resume for a long time, she continued to study. I was glad she did. Even if med school never happened, the knowledge she was acquiring could still make her a doctor and potentially save lives, ours particularly.

I leaned over the top of her and snuggled her neck. Her hair smelled like stale, days-old fruity shampoo. I drank it in because it was her.

She got up and followed me to the door to slide the three 2×6s into the security brackets after I left. "Be careful out there."

"I will. See you in a bit." I threw on my empty backpack, opened the door, pushed my bike out, then closed the door quickly behind me. She still felt the blast of arctic air rush through the open door. "Good-bye, Love. Brrrrr! So cold!" I heard her slide the boards into place with a soft thud for each. Standing outside on the wood porch I couldn't see a light on inside. All the windows were shuttered on the inside with scrap lumber from houses in the neighborhood that had been blown up. Destroyed homes also provided a lot of fuel for burning. Wisps of smoke from our chimney were the only visible signs of life coming from our home.

The cold instantly attacked me and tried to penetrate my layers. Once I wheeled my bike outside, the cold began to affect it immediately too. The cold thickened the grease in the pedal crank. Constant pedaling would help keep it loose, but it would never stay warm at this temperature. The sooner I got on and rode the better the bike would function. I continuously pedaled two blocks through the six inches of snow on the road we lived on, until I hit Third Street, a more-traveled, snow-packed road through the heart of downtown.

The frigid wind was relentless. Even with all my layers, the cold quickly broke through to feel cool on my arms and hands. This was the coldest night I had ever ridden, and I wasn't completely sure it could be done, but we were running low on fish and meat, and who knew when we would get more canned stuff from the government.

I was breaking curfew, and I was hoping the cold would keep the patrols indoors.

Who in their right mind would be out on a night like this, especially on a bicycle?

The immediate chill subsided, as my blood flowed faster. I wasn't warm, but my muscles had loosened up and the flow of endorphins put me in a familiar groove.

A car drove by as I passed through downtown. It was packed, and all eyes were on me.

What the hell are you looking at?

I didn't know why they were out. Maybe they were looking for food, or maybe the car was their only refuge from the cold. If they were hungry, hopefully they weren't too hungry.

I patted my chest to reassure myself that my holstered 9 mm was inside my coat.

They drove on.

I rode for blocks and I didn't see another vehicle. It was quiet except for my own breathing and the annoying, persistent wind blowing past my muffled ears.

This must be what it's like to be the last man on earth.

I didn't want to be the last man, although it was possible.

Most of the streetlights were out on the Causeway, but the intermittent few that were on reflected off the snow and lit up the night around me. I passed a woman sitting on the bus stop bench, stiff as a sculpture. The buses stopped running months ago. It had been about three weeks since I made this ride, and she wasn't there before.

I rode past Taco Tommy's, now dark and vacant. It was halfway to my destination and the bridge two blocks away, spanning four sets of railroad tracks, was the next leg of the ride. It was a grind to get to the top of the bridge and so far, the hardest part of the ride. As I headed down the other side, I saw a patrol truck three blocks ahead. It crossed east to west on Clinton Street and was gone. I didn't think they saw me, but I couldn't take any chances, so at the bottom of the bridge I took a right then a quick left down an alley and ducked behind a garage. The still of winter was dead quiet. As I listened for the patrol truck, I noticed a few houses emitting dim light. The smell of burning wood permeated the air.

After a few minutes—it seemed longer than that—I went north down the alley. The only tracks in the snow were the ones I was making. The virgin snow was deep and a slog to ride through. I got back onto the Causeway and headed to the restaurant where I used to work.

My hands and feet were cold by the time I pulled up around the back of the building. I unlocked the door and walked into the kitchen with my bike. Although there was no power and no heat, it was still warmer than being out in the wind. I pulled my flashlight out of my bag and lit up the kitchen. It was a moment literally frozen in time.

Two months ago, on a late November afternoon, a solar storm hit Earth. I was watching the Packers game while Winnie was studying at the kitchen table. "What the hell?"

"What happened?" Winnie's study lamp went out.

"Power's out." I tried to go on the Internet with my phone to get updates on the game, but it didn't work. "Can you get online with your phone?"

"No." And about the same time there was a loud *Boom!* Winnie and I ran outside and heard multiple explosions going off in the city. We watched plumes of dark smoke rise from the blasts as the ground shook. There was an explosion every few seconds, some distant, some near, until the closest blast took out the house at the end of the block. It knocked Winnie and me to the ground, but we got up right away and stumbled into the street. I thought we were under attack. Police cars, fire trucks, and other emergency vehicle sirens screamed from all directions.

People realized that it wasn't safe being inside, so they funneled into the street on this cold fall day.

"We have to get our coats," I said. Winnie and I ran back inside. We raced around the house frantically gathering our things. Along with our winter coats, hats, and gloves, we grabbed our wallets, laptops, and finally our bikes on the way out the door. Winnie also grabbed her backpack and textbooks. I grabbed our guns. "Go! Go! Go! Get out!" As Winnie ran out the door, I dashed back into the kitchen and grabbed the peanut butter, bread, and milk. In the moment, I wondered if I would feel it.

God, please don't blow me up! Even though I didn't know whether God existed, or whether the existence was even benevolent, it felt like a good idea to acknowledge the possibility that something other than my own actions could save my life.

"Hurry, Love!" Winnie yelled from the street.

I launched myself out of the house so violently with my bike the screen door banged against the house with a *Crack!* so loud that the crowd of neighbors in the street scattered.

Winnie and I rode our bikes three blocks to Houska Park along the Mississippi River to get away from exploding houses and buildings. Other people had the same idea. Most were in their warm cars.

Winnie and I stared at them enviously. "Do you think someone will let us sit in their car with them?" Winnie asked.

"I don't know. Don't think so. I don't think we should if they do," I said.

When society breaks down, trust for people diminishes until outright paranoia takes over.

We gathered small branches and collected burnable garbage from the trash cans to build a fire in a park grill. When we heard an explosion near our neighborhood, we said, "I wonder if that was our house." Eventually we stopped saying it, but still thinking it.

I ate my peanut butter sandwich and wondered if we would have to spend the night here. Late afternoon soon became dusk at this time of year in Wisconsin.

"I don't want to sleep outside," Winnie said.

As we huddled together on a picnic table that we pulled up to our fire, we heard a roar in the sky. Winnie and I watched a passenger jet fall like a missile and crash into the bluffs at the edge of the city. We wanted to feel bad for all those people who died, but as the sun went down, we were desperately concerned about our own lives.

Over the next three hours the explosions gradually decreased until they stopped. We waited another hour before we rode back home with no idea whether we had a place to live. As we turned back onto our street, Winnie saw it first, "It's there! Oh my God, it's there! Our home is still there, Love!"

Still, this was the beginning of the end of the world as we knew it.

Once radio and TV stations, and cell phone towers that had off-grid generator systems, came back online, we learned that the electrical charge from the solar storm blew up gas and oil lines (thus the building explosions), severely damaged power stations, disabled cell phone towers, wrecked satellites, and caused core meltdowns in nuclear power plants. Airplanes flying above 30,000 feet were exposed to the brunt of the storm. Thousands had plummeted to the earth, and I was surprised that we had only seen one fall.

Martial law ensued, and the President came on about once a day for a few minutes to address the nation about what the government was doing to bring aid. Still, three months after the solar storm electricity was limited to a few hours a day and came and went without notice. Natural gas still wasn't available. We lived in an old house that was converted into a duplex years ago, and we were lucky enough to have a fireplace in our small living room. With houses splintered by explosions there was plenty to burn.

Our neighbors in the duplex, a family of four, left a couple of weeks after the solar storm. A limo and two escorting SUVs drove up and took them away. I didn't know who it was, but someone of means rescued them. Like always, those with money were protected from this catastrophe. Winnie and I looted any food they had left.

Those with the least get hurt the most. It is the fundamental order in a world with a god who has no preference.

There was no one to rescue us. After we got the limited cell phone service, I was able to talk to my mother. When the storm hit, she told me she immediately drove to my aunt's farm. I guess most of the family, except those that died from the storm, had the same idea. The idea crossed my mind too, but Winnie and I didn't think a thirty-five-mile bike ride in danger and chaos was a good plan at the time. Now that martial law was imposed, only vehicles to transport food, medicine, or anything considered an emergency were allowed on highways.

Winnie had no family in town. She was from Iowa. Her father and I had a short conversation about the guns I had. "Winnie can shoot," he said.

"I know."

But the question in my mind was, *Can she kill. Can I?*

ON THE DAY OF THE STORM, I was scheduled to work so I did show up. I knew the restaurant, like everywhere else, would have been thrown into chaos when the storm hit. There was a good possibility that it was gone.

Winnie made the ride with me. Both of us brought our 9 mms, tucked in our shoulder holsters inside our winter coats.

We rode through streets that were littered with debris from exploded buildings and houses. Traffic was heavy and frantic. We rode past the Superfoods Grocery Store where there was a strong police presence. Red and blue flashing lights lit up the entire area. It wouldn't be long before hunger would cause bloody battles in supermarket parking lots.

I wheeled my bike in through the back of the restaurant like I always did, but this time Winnie followed. "Just stay by the door with the bikes, okay?"

"Sure, Love," she said nervously and pulled out her gun.

I walked through the empty kitchen. The dishwasher had been abandoned with trays and tubs of dirty dishes piled near it. The counters and floor were a mess. I made a quick walk through to make sure no one was here. The restaurant was dimly lit by the battery-powered lights. I used the flashlight app on my phone to see better. I had my gun drawn in my other hand. In the dining room the tables had plates of food and beverages that people had left. The shelves in the bar had been emptied of the booze. I went back to the kitchen and to the office in there. I grabbed one of the two sets of keys that hung next to the door. The other set was gone.

I had been stealing from the restaurant for almost the entire time I worked there. I cleaned the place at night when no one else was there. Before the morning crew arrived, I went into the cooler and took some meat, usually about a pound of ground beef, but occasionally I took some Cod or a couple of steaks. I stole about twice a week. All employees got a free meal during their shift, and I could have gotten a free breakfast in the morning, but I rarely did. I took my share my own way, and I justified it because the pay was shitty. Looting was going to be the way of the world for the foreseeable future, and I guess I had a head start.

I unlocked the walk-in cooler like I had before, and I was surprised to see how much was left. It probably wouldn't be long before who-ever had the other keys would be back, so Winnie and I stuffed our backpacks with as much meat and fish as we could. We also grabbed a heavy-duty kitchen garbage bag and put as many industrial sized cans of fruit, vegetables, baked beans, and chocolate pudding as we could carry and still ride our bikes. This was the hardest ride to the restaurant, until I rode on the coldest day in the dead of winter.

Every time I made the ride I wondered if someone had discovered the food in the cooler, but no one else had. I questioned whether the others who had a key to the cooler were still alive. Not that a key was necessary to get in; a bolt cutter could snap the lock easily.

The restaurant had no power, but the subzero temps kept every-thing in the cooler frozen. That was the only good thing about the cold, and I wondered if I would get everything out before spring.

After I loaded my backpack, I called Winnie. "I'm heading back, Win."

"Did you get much?"

"Backpack is stuffed. I still don't think anyone's been here except us."

"That's great!"

"I'll see you when I get home."

"Be careful. I love you."

"Love you. Bye."

Winnie and I never talked like it could be the last time, and we never belabored our good-byes.

The ride back to the Causeway was uneventful, except the frozen woman on the park bench was gone. Food was scarce, but it hadn't come to this for Winnie and me yet.

I cursed the wind in my face on the ride there, and now I was so glad the wind was at my back. The weight of the backpack made my shoulders and spine ache. The fatigue made me colder. My toes were numb, but my fingers weren't as bad. The rest of my body was slowly breaking down from the surreal freezing temp. I was heading through downtown and in the homestretch, only about five minutes from home, so I wasn't concerned, until the same car I saw earlier turned the corner and slowly headed toward me.

As the car slowly passed me, I saw a dozen starving eyes through frosty windows staring at me. I unzipped my coat to get to my gun. The steely subzero air rushed in and stabbed me in the chest. I glanced back. At the corner, the car was making a U-turn.

Why?! Why?! Why?!

As I continued to ride, I pulled my left mitten off and stuffed it in my coat pocket. I put my left hand on my gun inside my coat and rested it there. Riding one handed usually wasn't a problem, but the road was snow packed and almost as slippery as ice.

I took the left side of the road, and the car slowly passed me again. The driver's window came down. "Pretty damn cold to be out riding a bike, man!" he yelled. He had a messy beard and a dirty red and white Wisconsin Badger's stocking cap pulled tightly around his ears.

"I'm almost home. Have a good night."

The window in the back came down and a young woman with a blaze orange winter hunting hat asked, "What's in the backpack?"

I could see two sets of eyes on either side of her. "Clothes." I lied. I knew they wouldn't believe me, but I needed an answer.

"Stop for a second," she said.

"No, I just want to get home," I said. I was waiting for them to say something about my hand inside my jacket. Sometimes people are unaware of the obvious, blinded by emotion, desire, or sensation. Hunger was probably their distraction.

The car sped ahead then pulled across the road to block my path at the corner by the Hollywood Theatre. I pulled out my gun and pointed it at them and fired twice. Gunshots are so loud, even outdoors. I felt deaf for a second. Then I heard some yelling and the car spun away, sliding all over the road. Soon it was down the block and gone.

I thought my hand was shaking from the cold when I put my gun away, but my heart was also racing from the past few violent seconds. Still, I wasn't sure why my hand shook so bad. I shivered, and my teeth chattered, as I zipped up my coat. I knew bullets hit the car, but I didn't want to hurt anyone, kill anyone. I just wanted to get home to Winnie with our food.

I pedaled the last three blocks with little left in me. My body was stiff and exhausted from the ride, and my spirit was damaged by all the moments along the way. I banged on the door. "Winnie! It's me!"

Open the door. Please.

As I took off my mittens to pull out my phone and call Winnie, the car I had shot at roared around the corner and plowed toward me. At the moment, among the many frenetic thoughts spinning through my mind, I wished I had given them the backpack. Maybe they would have been satisfied—then again, maybe not. Maybe I should have fired shots through their windows before when I had the chance and tried to hit someone. Once again, I didn't want to kill anyone, but right now as the car was bearing down on me I was thinking that was a mistake.

The deep snow on the street made the car swerve and its wheels spin. Before I had a chance to do anything, the car slid to a stop and two handguns stuck out from the backseat open window on the driver's side and began firing. I ducked down to make myself small and used my bike and a post on the porch for cover. At that moment the cold in my bones temporarily disappeared. The fear of freezing to death was masked by the terror of gunshots.

As I struggled to pull out my 9 mm, Winnie cracked open the door and fired back with the AR-15. She steadied the barrel against the door jam and emptied the thirty-round magazine into the car. Her first shots went through the back seat open window and silenced any gunfire coming from the car. When the car tried to pull away, Winnie continued to fire, and the other bullets tore through the front seat.

The car stopped in its tracks with the engine still running. Otherwise, there wasn't a sound or movement.

I scampered into the house on my hands and knees, threw off the backpack, and rolled onto my back. Winnie bolted the door behind me. "Love, are you okay?"

"I'm not shot, if that's what you mean. Where were you? Why didn't you answer the door?"

"I was going to the bathroom. I didn't hear you knock." She sat down beside me and grabbed my hand. "So cold." Her lips quivered, and her eyes welled up. I wasn't sure if she was crying because she thought she almost lost me, or because she just shot up a car full of people. It was probably both.

My glasses were now fogged up from coming in from the cold to the warmth. Winnie let me use the hem of her shirt to wipe them off. Then I crawled to the window and peeked through a crack between the boards. "The car's on fire."

Winnie crouched beside me to look for herself. Together we watched the car become engulfed in flames. We quietly watched for any movement and listened for any sound. There wasn't anything.

"How many?" Winnie asked. Her voice cracked and she began to sob.

"I don't know," I said, but I knew there were at least four people in the car. I pulled her close to me. "You had to. They tried to kill me. They wanted to take everything we have."

"I guess we can't leave the world to people like them," she said.

"No, we can't." But I knew there was a fine line between them and us, and what we were becoming.

Retaliatory Strike Force

GARTH UPSHAW

> Garth Upshaw lives in Portland, Oregon, with his
> wife and three super-genius children. His work has
> appeared in *Clarkesworld*, *Beneath Ceaseless Skies*,
> *Realms of Fantasy*, and other fine venues. His
> passions include drawing, carving spoons, space,
> and all aspects of the bizarre. "Retaliatory Strike
> Force" is original to *Bullet Points*.

THE BUS LURCHED around a pothole, throwing me sideways. I stumbled onto a woman's foot. "Sorry." I have reflexes like a cobra. "Hey, driver. Where'd you get your license? A cereal box?" I yukked it up. "Someone could get hurt." The other passengers looked away.

"It's a bot." The woman cocked her head at me. "There isn't a driver." All her clothes were grimy and patched—like mine, but I was sloppier with a needle.

I raised my hand. "Call coming in. Implant." I touched the side of my head. "Yeah? What's the happen?" I strode up the narrow aisle. On fire. "Yeah. I have the address. Right here." I slapped my chest pocket. "Huh. No shit. Remember lifting those cycles? We kicked up a dust plume you could see from orbit."

I snapped my fingers and leaned toward the woman. "I was on Mars. You know that?" I pointed at my own face. Gray warehouses scrolled by outside. "Karl." Plebes huddled in doorways or gathered around barrel fires.

The woman frowned at me. "I had a brother on Mars. 31st Tele-bots. New Bangkok. '43." Her voice got very quiet.

"That was bad." I grabbed a support bar, flipped upside down, and thumped the roof with my boots.*Bam!* "We'll get them damn zooks."

A bored voice crackled through the speakers. "Remain calm, sir. Disrespecting bus property carries a 1,000-mark penalty."

"Penalize this, you useless seat warmer." I flipped the camera off. Big honking finger up its ass. "You maggots'd be speaking Chinese if it wasn't for grunts like me. You show some respect."

"Karl Miller?" The woman's eyes widened with recognition. "Central High? Jenny Weintraub."

"Just Karl. Karl-nothing-else." This Karl had been newborn on Mars. "I was left for dead on the tallest fucking mountain in the universe. Olympic Mons. Ha. Pussy mountain. We made some jokes, let me tell you." Bright lights around a corpclave sparkled off razor wire.

"They ship you back?"

"I gotta job." I lowered my voice. "Undercover. FBI." I touched my nose. "The zooks have spies everywhere." The bus swerved again. I fell onto a man sitting by the window. His hat flew off, exposing dark black hair. I grabbed his arm. "Hey. Where are you from?"

"Here. I was born here." The man shrank away from me, but his dusky skin and slanted eyes gave me all the information I needed.

I yanked him to his feet. "Yeah? Yeah? Does a straight beat a flush?"

He gabbled and twisted like a landed fish. "I'm no spy."

The speakers crackled to life. "Release your fellow passenger."

"He's a goddamn zook." I wrapped my hand in his shirt and power lifted him. Ha!

"Release the passenger." The snout of a ceiling-mounted autotangle gun swiveled toward me.

Jenny touched my elbow. "Put him down, Karl."

"Down? Down?" I got right in the man's face. Bits of spittle flew from my mouth. "You want down, buddy?"

The gun coughed one-two-three. Pain enveloped me like a living blanket. Like my skin had leaped off my body, exposing every nerve to sandpaper. I saw flashes of bright light. I passed out.

I WOKE ON A PLASTIC BENCH at the transit station. Drizzle fell from a leaden sky. My head pounded. Every muscle in my body felt like it'd been rolled in powdered glass.

An ad board flickered to life. Laughing, healthy models held out bottles of Old Granddad. "Only two blocks south. On sale today." Their teeth gleamed.

I forced myself upright. "Don't need your gut-rot crap. I have the address." I slapped my chest. It hurt.

"Karl?" Jenny's voice took me by surprise.

I whirled around. She was sitting on the bench. My head felt ten sizes too big. "What the hell are you doing here?"

She shrugged. "This was my stop. I convinced the transit cops you wouldn't cause any more trouble." She chewed her lip. "You remind me of my brother."

"Damn zooks." I looked behind me. "I was in the retaliatory strike force. Eye for an eye."

Jenny was quiet. The ad board spouted a tinny jingle. A pigeon cocked its head at a candy wrapper.

I staggered toward the half flight of stairs to the street. "Zoom, zoom. Gotta go. Got the address."

"What address?" Jenny stood up.

"Wife and kids." I stumbled forward. Jenny put her hand out. All at once, I was back in the tunnels. Twisting permacrete passages. The rush of my O_2 breather hot on my face. Lights flashed. Dust coated my tongue. Wires sparked. The scent of ozone tainted the air.

I leaped forward. "Zooks to the right." I spun. My hand lashed out in a killing blow. A soft crunch. A gasp.

"Karl." Jenny's agonized face seemed to appear out of nowhere just centimeters from mine. She coughed. A trickle of blood leaked from her mouth.

My implant buzzed. "Sorry. Gotta call." I touched my jaw.

Jenny's eyes glazed over. "Karl."

The skin along my chin was rough with stubble. No implant scar. The buzzing in my head grew to a roar.

Jenny sagged to the ground. My fist uncurled. I wanted the sharp, clean anger of war, but all I could find inside was emptiness. I scrabbled at the sheet of paper in my pocket. Blank. But I knew that.

A bus pulled up to the curb, and the doors hissed open. Street lights flickered on and lit the platform in smoky orange circles. I bent to check Jenny's pulse. "Call an ambulance, damn it." A new Karl needed to be born. Now. Ice-cold rain fell on my face.

Review: *Rogue Sequence*, by Zac Topping

NATHAN W. TORONTO

Zac Topping spent his formative years on the move, as some do, and it was in the fifth grade where he found an outlet for his active imagination through writing. After high school he joined the U.S. Army, where he served in an artillery unit out of Fort Bragg (now Fort Liberty). He served for four-and-a-half years, with two tours in Iraq. He currently lives with his wife in a quiet farm town in Connecticut and is a firefighter for the city he grew up in. *Rogue Sequence* is available wherever books are sold.

WE WERE DUE for a character like Ander Rade in military science fiction, an anti-hero whose power, depth, and complexity can carry not one but many novels. Zac Topping's *Rogue Sequence* starts with a pulse-pounding prologue and gets even better from there, intertwining satisfying character arcs and giving just the right number of twists to keep the reader guessing until the very last page. Topping has given us a story that melds Jack Reacher with the Terminator. The result leaves the reader wanting more Rade. Much more.

The premise of *Rogue Sequence* is intriguing. Rade is a genetically modified mercenary who is betrayed on a black op, then spends years behind bars, but gets let out to hunt down the former teammate who betrayed him. He starts out motivated by revenge and the promise of freedom, but the twisted plots and subplots he uncovers on his frenetic journey force him to reexamine everything he thought he knew about himself.

Rogue Sequence earns five bullets because it goes well beyond a compelling thriller with a captivating main character. This novel explores fundamental issues of human existence in a world where genetic modification and cyborg manipulation are everyday tech and government is beholden to a myriad of cynical corporate interests. How does modifying genes change our humanity? What is the appropriate role for enhanced humans in managing violence? How do we build bridges of understanding and empathy with the genetic outcasts of society?

If these questions resonate with our world today, then I suspect that was Topping's design. The best military science fiction points a microscope at how we manage war and violence in the real world. That Topping does this so effortlessly in *Rogue Sequence* is a testament not only to his keen assessment of life today but also to his ability to weave gritty, authentic combat experiences into a story set dozens of years in the future.

It is also worth noting that Topping has built a compelling world, a point I zinged him on in reviewing his first novel. The world he builds in *Rogue Sequence*, in contrast, is not only gritty and authentic, but also disturbingly plausible. He blends just the right amount of incremental technological development with political changes that are so unexpected that they suggest that black swans really can happen. It's not a world I would build in my own mind, but it is utterly believable coming from his.

Bullet Points does not review a book unless it is worthy of at least four bullets. A four-bullet review means that a serious reader of military science fiction should definitely check out the sample and make their own decision about a purchase. Five bullets mean that a book deserves to be bought and read post-haste. If nothing else, doing this for Topping's *Rogue Sequence* might help us prevent the dark and frightening world he paints from coming about.

Also from BULLET POINT PRESS

SAGA OF THE EMERALD MOON
Nathan W. Toronto

Rise of Ahrik

Revenge of the Emerald Moon

Redemption of the White Planet
(coming soon)

BULLET POINTS
Nathan W. Toronto, ed.

Volumes 1–5

Subscribe to *Bullet Points*